EVERY CAKE HAS A STORY

by CHRISTINA TOSI of MILK BAR®

illustrated by EMILY BALSLEY

 Dial Books for Young Readers

The day was black and white and gray.
It was always the same gray on Samesday.
The trees, the houses, the doors, the dogs, the clothes,
and the people were all the same too.
Everything was the same in Samesville.

In her family's kitchen, Sammi wondered what cake to make.
The answer was the same as always: vanilla with chocolate frosting.
Sammi loved vanilla cake, but it never ever changed.

Before she went to bed,
Sammi placed her recipe
card under her pillow.

"I wish things were NOT
the same," Sammi said
into the world.

That night her dreams were NEW and WILD
and everything in between!

When Sammi woke up, she remembered her wish.
The cake recipe!

But under her pillow there wasn't just one recipe anymore.
There was a book! And not just any book.

A cookbook!
Full of cakes and colors,
and ingredients she'd never seen.

This was what the world could be!

MAGICAL
WORLD
OF LAYER
CAKES

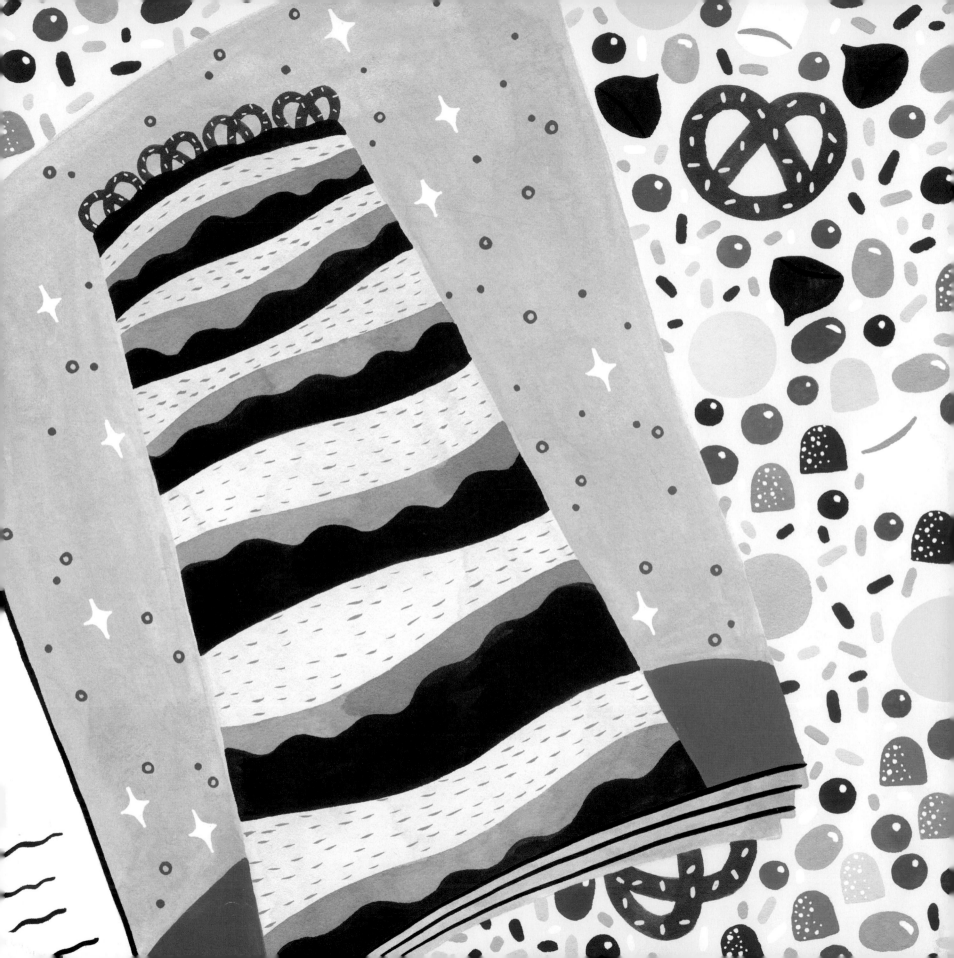

Sammi rushed outside.
The trees, the houses, the doors, the dogs, the clothes, and the people were all different now.
This was no longer Samesville.
This was somewhere amazing!

Everyone was an individual.

Everyone was unique.

Everyone was having fun in their own way.

Then Sammi had an idea!

Sammi and her friends rushed into the kitchen.
It was time to bake another cake, but this time it wouldn't be vanilla.

Sammi shouted out ingredients,
and her friends worked the line.

Sammi had dreamed up a cake that was as different as can be. A cake full of colors and flavors. A cake that told the story of the new world around them. Beautiful and individual, just like Sammi and her friends.

And she knew one thing for sure . . .

Things would NEVER be the same again.

DREAMY STRAWBERRY FROSTING

Makes 2 cups

1 stick of butter, softened

¼ cup powdered sugar

¼ cup strawberry jam

tiny pinch of kosher salt

Starting on low speed, use a mixer to combine your butter and powdered sugar for 3 minutes. Add in your jam and salt, increase the mixer to medium speed, and whip until super fluffy, about 3 minutes. Spread on cake of your choosing!

To the Derris family and their love of cake, and of stories.
And to every Sammi out there, looking to bring color
and flavor to life in the kitchen. –C.T.

To Stella, who finds joy in doing her own thing. –E.B.

Dial Books for Young Readers
An imprint of Penguin Random House LLC, New York

First published in the United States of America by Dial Books for Young Readers, an imprint of Penguin Random House LLC, 2021

Text copyright © 2021 by Christina Tosi
Illustrations copyright © 2021 by Emily Balsley

Visit us online at penguinrandomhouse.com.

Library of Congress Cataloging-in-Publication Data is available.

Manufactured in China
ISBN 9780593110683

1 3 5 7 9 10 8 6 4 2

Design by Jennifer Kelly • Text set in Avenir
The art for this book was created using gouache and ink, composited in Photoshop.